THE ADVENTURES OF
NOUN & VERB

WRITTEN BY LAWRENCE PIERRE
ILLUSTRATED BY DEJA DAMERON

THE ADVENTURES OF NOUN & VERB

EDITED BY LANGSTON A. PIERRE

SPECIAL THANKS TO...
LYLA
JAXON
JULIETTE PIERRE
AND GUSTAVE LEBRIS

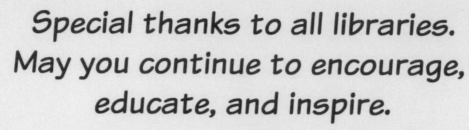
Special thanks to all libraries.
May you continue to encourage,
educate, and inspire.

Once upon a time in a *far, far land...*

Noun met Verb and they were the best of friends!

Noun knew every **person**, **place**, and **thing**!

Noun can be a
doctor...

A pilot...

...or even **a shoe**!

Noun can be anything!
A Noun can be
YOU!

Noun and Verb were
SUPER FRIENDS!

Now, let the story begin...

Noun and Verb went on a quest to **Parts Of Speech Land.** Verb asked Noun...

Noun already had a plan to get to **Principal Langston.**

Noun and Verb finally arrived to **Parts Of Speech Land**. They met **Principal Langston** at **Pronoun Elementary**. **Suzie Slang** and **Poor Grammar George** had failing grades and were acting a fool. He asked them to help Suzie and George improve in school.

Suzie Slang was rude. She always had detention in school. She said "ain't" all the time and could not play at recess.

She always said bad words and failed all her test, but Verb knew Suzie could change if she tried her best.

Her partner in class was *Poor Grammar George*. He thought school was boring and only for nerds. Poor Grammar George was big tall and mean. He always yelled, he always screamed.

They both agreed, curious of the Noun and Verb team. Poor Grammar George said, "I act mean and tough because I eat Cheese Puffs and Google stuff. I want to learn how to write and read to be a **smarter ME.**"

Noun and Verb **ran.** Suzie Slang and Poor Grammar George both **danced.** They now felt brand new! They wanted to be a part of the **Library Crew!**

It was the place you could have fun in peace. The Library is full of endless possibilities!

You can learn about trees and learn to read.

Mission accomplished! Noun and Verb was happy as can be!
They all shouted "Knowledge is Power!" outside the library...

...while Principal Langston smiled because in education, he always believed.

34980748R00015

Made in the USA
Middletown, DE
06 February 2019